For Ray, the captain

www.dragonbloodpirates.co.uk

ORCHARD BOOKS
338 Euston Road, London NW1 3BH

First published in 2008 by Lothian Children's Books,
an imprint of Hachette Livre Australia
First published in the UK in 2011 by Orchard Books

ISBN 978 1 40830 824 0

Text © Dan Jerris 2008
Skull, crossbones and ragged parchment image © Brendon De Suza
Map illustrations on pages 4–5 © Rory Walker, 2008
All other illustrations © Orchard Books 2011

A CIP catalogue record for this book is available from the British Library.

10 9 8 7 6 5 4 3 2 1

Printed in Great Britain by CPI Bookmarque, Croydon

Orchard Books is a division of Hachette Children's Books,
an Hachette UK company.

www.hachette.co.uk

The Golden Casket

Dan Jerris

ORCHARD BOOKS

abre Island

Town

Dragon's Stomach

Snake Island

Ghost Island.

Dragon Blood Islands

Pirate Mateys and Scallywags

Alleric (Al) Breas: Lives in Drake Drive and owns a mysterious sea trunk that takes him to the Dragon Blood Islands

Blacktooth McGee: A very nasty pirate who runs the brigantine *The Revenge*

Demon Dan: An evil pirate who died on Dragon Island and whose black diamond became stuck between a dragon's teeth

Evil Pearl: A deathless pirate who becomes Queen of Pearl Island and sacrifices people to a sea monster

Flash Johnny: Blacktooth's devious and greedy cabin boy

Grandfather: Mahoot's grandfather and guardian of the swimming elephants on Sabre Island

Greeny Joe: A shark so big and old that mould grows on his skin, making him glow green in the dark

Grenda: Snotty Nell's daughter

Gunner: The pirate captain of the ship *The Invincible*

Halimeda (Hally) Breas: Al's younger sister

Mahoot: Captain Gunner's cabin boy

Mozzy: *The Invincible*'s bosun – small and fast

Joe Seabrook: Al's best friend

Pigface McNurt: Blacktooth's bosun; a huge pirate with a ring through his nose

Prince Alleric: The prince who once ruled Sabre Island but disappeared in mysterious circumstances

Princess Haree: The princess of Ruby Island

Razor Toe: A deathless pirate who has enslaved the people of Ruby Island

Sharkbait: Snotty Nell's one-legged bosun

Slicer: *The Invincible*'s cook

Snakeboot: A magical white three-legged cat with purple eyes. Legend has it he once belonged to a terrifying pirate called Vicious Victor.

Snotty Nell: A horrible one-eyed pirate who sails a worn-out Indiaman called *Nausi VIII*

Stanley Spong: A crooked, sneaky trader in town who cheats people

Vampire Zu: Snotty Nell's huge first mate

Velvetfoot: A fearsome pirate distinctive for his velvet shoes that let him creep up on his victims unannounced

Vicious Victor: A pirate ghost. He used to pillage the Dragon Blood Islands and stole the magical sabre and scabbard that belonged to Prince Alleric.

The Scabbard of Invincibility

"Ow! That hurt," Al Breas complained, rubbing his arm.

"Sorry," said his best friend, Jack Seabrook, "but you did say to hit you hard."

"I thought I wouldn't feel any pain," said Al. "I thought the Scabbard of Invincibility with its new dragon diamond would protect me."

Their three-legged white cat, Snakeboot,

sat on an old sea trunk beside Al. He reached out with his paw and his claws caught on the glittering black diamond set in the silver scabbard hanging from Al's waist. Al unhooked the cat's claw and studied the sheath and jewel with a worried frown.

"Mahoot's grandfather said you'd have to find all four black dragon diamonds and put them back on the scabbard before it can make you invincible," Jack reminded Al.

"So, at the moment, if I'm wearing the scabbard and get knifed in the guts, I'll still be wounded," said Al, shivering at the thought.

"Yes, but you won't die unless you take the scabbard off," said Jack. "The diamond on the scabbard makes you deathless."

Al shuddered at the memory of the diamond's last owner, Razor Toe the pirate king. He had crumbled to dust when the black diamond he wore in his turban was

snatched from his head. Now the same
diamond that Razor Toe had worn glittered
from Al's scabbard.

"I don't want to end up like Razor Toe,"
said Al.

Snakeboot meowed, left the sea trunk and wound himself around Al's legs in agreement.

"Razor Toe was bad enough," said Jack, "but when we return to the Dragon Blood Islands with the sabre and scabbard, Blacktooth will want to steal them from us, too."

"What should we do?" said Al. "I do want to go back to the islands, but I'm worried…"

"Let's leave the sabre and scabbard here then," Jack suggested. He bent down and tickled Snakeboot's ear. "What do you think, Snakeboot? Should we leave them behind?"

The cat arched his back and purred loudly in answer, then leapt to the top of an old cupboard.

"I think he wants us to put them up there," said Jack. "They'd be out of reach of your little sister. Hally will never see them up there."

Al unbuckled his weapon and sheath,

climbed on a chair and placed them on top of the cupboard, away from prying eyes.

"I suppose that'll be fine," said Al, "since Vicious Victor gave us rings, too." He held out his hand to regard the ruby-eyed dragonhead ring, a gift from the pirate ghost, that glittered on his thumb. "We have to find out what they're all about."

"Who would have guessed my ring once belonged to Princess Haree of Ruby Island?" said Jack. "Or that it was a key to secret passageways? Maybe your dragon ring, Hally's pearl ring and Mahoot's elephant-head ring have secrets too."

"We know Vicious Victor wants Snakeboot to help us find Prince Alleric's lost treasures so he can finally rest in peace," Al replied, "so the rings may be keys to more treasures."

Snakeboot purred loudly and his purple eyes flashed, as if agreeing with Al. He went to the sea trunk and pawed at the lock.

"OK, that's settled then," said Jack. "I think Snakeboot's saying it's time for us to return to the Dragon Blood Islands."

Snakeboot purred again, so Al opened the sea trunk and stepped inside. Jack and the cat followed. In seconds they had vanished from Al's attic at number five Drake Drive.

Finding themselves back on Ruby Island, Al and Jack discovered that Captain Gunner and the crew of *The Dandylion* had been so busy celebrating their victory over Razor Toe that they hadn't missed the boys at all. Breathing sighs of relief, they settled back into the festivities.

A few days later, celebrations complete, a cheering crowd lined the docks as *The Dandylion* cast off and set course for the main town in the Dragon Blood Islands. Al and Jack stood on the poop deck with Gunner and their friend, Mahoot, the cabin boy, waving goodbye.

"I'm glad the king of Ruby Island is back on the throne," said Al.

"And that we sent Blacktooth running," chortled Captain Gunner. "Now I'm gunner buy some big cannons so I can blast him to kingdom come next time we see him."

"Where do you reckon Blacktooth's gone?" asked Mahoot. "He took off like a frightened rabbit when Razor Toe crumbled to dust."

"That lisping lickspittle might attack us again, especially now he knows Al's got the Dragon Blood Sabre," said Gunner. He glanced at Al's waist, looking for the sabre, and his eyebrows shot up in surprise. "Where is it?" he cried in alarm. "You haven't gone and lost it, have you?"

"Don't worry," replied Al. "I've hidden it where no one can find it."

The Treasure

While Captain Gunner was fitting new cannons to *The Dandylion* below decks, Stanley Spong shuffled up the gangplank. Al and Jack, curious as to why the shifty trader would come aboard, took him straight down to Gunner.

"What are you doing here?" asked Gunner, eyeing Spong suspiciously.

Spong shuffled his feet, coughed and spat. He looked sideways at Gunner, not meeting his eyes. "I've got some information for you," he said. "And it might be worth a bit."

"Tempt me," said Gunner, intrigued.

Spong's voice dropped. "Blacktooth and Snotty are both in port, and Blacktooth's hurrying to finish a special bit of work he's having done on *The Revenge* so he can leave as quickly as possible tomorrow. He knows about something that Snotty does too, and he's planning to get there first."

"What something?" asked Gunner.

"Treasure," Spong replied. "And as I'm the only one who can tell you what they know, I want a bit of the booty you've already found for myself."

Gunner reached into his pocket and pulled out a small ruby. "This is the best you'll get from me," he said, holding out the gem.

"One small ruby for a golden casket full of sapphires?" whispered Spong, and waited for Gunner to digest the bait.

"One more then — but that's it," Gunner offered. "And the information had better be good, especially as Snotty and Blacktooth already know about it."

"So you'd be happy to let them get it all for themselves and not even try to get it yourself, would you?" asked Spong, knowing full well Gunner held a big grudge against both the other pirates — a grudge big enough to make him race them to any treasure.

Gunner grabbed another ruby. "Here, take this, and tell me what they know," he growled. The ruby sparkled in his hand and Spong's eyes flashed greedily as he took the payment, before reaching into his coat and handing Gunner two pages torn from a book. "I found this old diary that belonged to a butler who once worked in Prince Alleric's castle on Sabre Island. The man is dead, of course, and his granddaughter has been selling all his things.

These pages are all you need."

With those words Spong turned on his heels and rapidly left the boat.

Gunner pored over the pages, reading aloud: "Today Prince Alleric arrived home. Terrible news! His boat is badly damaged, half his crew are butchered, and his cargo and treasure are abandoned because of a terrible fight with Vicious Victor, the evil pirate who is ravaging the Dragon Blood Islands.

"Prince Alleric fought off the pirates, but as his boat was sinking under the weight of cargo he was forced to offload his freight, including a golden casket full of sapphires, on a deserted island. Then, almost single-handedly, the prince managed to sail his ruined boat home. Later, I overheard him tell his sister, Princess Halimeda, "I've made a map of the whereabouts of the golden casket. So that the map doesn't fall into the wrong hands, I've put it in the secret drawer inside

your elephant. Here is the key. Keep it safe."
He handed his sister a strange ring, shaped
like an elephant's head, and she put it on
her finger.

"Later, after the prince had repaired his
boat and was about to sail off again and
collect his treasure from the island, one of his
favourite elephants was injured. While the

prince was in the jungle helping the creature,
Vicious Victor arrived and ransacked Alleric
Castle. Princess Halimeda was robbed and
the ring was taken, along with lots of jewels
and treasure. The worst loss of all was Prince
Alleric's magical Dragon Blood Sabre and the
Scabbard of Invincibility.

"Afterwards, the prince sailed away, hoping

to get his revenge on Vicious Victor. He never returned, but I believe the map to the treasure can still be found in an elephant statue inside Alleric Castle..."

"Another key ring!" whispered Jack, staring at the elephant ring on Mahoot's finger. "Like the one I had, which opened secret doors."

"And one that was stolen by Vicious Victor," said Mahoot excitedly. "It might lead us to the lost casket of sapphires."

"We'll have to look lively if we want to catch tomorrow's tide and beat Snotty and Blacktooth to Sabre Island," said Gunner, interrupting the boys' whispered discussion.

"Who knows," said Mahoot cryptically, "we might have a bigger head start than we think."

The Death-giver

The Dandylion set sail the following afternoon in a brisk breeze, making good time until Mahoot, who was lookout in the crow's nest, called, "Sail! Dead ahead!"

Gunner fitted the telescope to his eye. "It's Snotty Nell, the old witch," he said, handing the telescope to Al. "Look for yourself. Why is she heading away from Sabre Island?"

"Sail!" cried Mahoot again. "Sail to starboard and closing fast!"

Al turned and picked up another boat

racing towards Snotty. "Blacktooth's after
her," he said, handing back the telescope.
"But his boat looks very strange."

"The cowardly wimp!" cried Gunner
as he sighted *The Revenge*. "He's fitted
a death-giver to his hull and Snotty's
running from him."

Suddenly, Snotty's ship *The Tormenter* made
a direct tack towards *The Dandylion*.

"The cunning old crow," Gunner growled.
"She's headed towards us and bringing
Blacktooth with her."

"What's a death-giver?" asked Jack.

His question was answered as *The Revenge*'s
prow was highlighted against the sun. On
either side of the hull, mounted through the
first gun-ports, were two huge metal blades,
making the ship look like a horned bull.

"Prepare for battle," ordered Gunner. "You
boys help Mozzy. Stack cutlasses under the
mast, prime the cannons and put the muskets

along the rails. We're about to fight for our lives!"

Soon the three boats were circling each other, tacking, making the most of the wind and looking for a weakness in their opponents' defences.

Mozzy, the bosun, took Mahoot and Jack below to help prime the twelve-pound cannons. They were soon collecting the powder cartridges from the forward magazine. "Being a powder monkey is really awful," groaned Mahoot, as he squeezed himself into the forward magazine and heaved the heavy bags of gunpowder up the narrow stairs to the cannon.

Meanwhile, Al brought shot and lead to the crew and raced up and down the decks, making sure everyone's muskets were ready.

Within minutes Snotty made her move, tacking between *The Dandylion* and *The*

Revenge, and forcing Blacktooth to come about as she stole his breeze. *The Tormenter* rolled heavily in the swell as Snotty fired her cannons. There was a booming explosion, but her aim was wide of the mark.

The Dandylion was now in Blacktooth's sights and he charged, his pirates screaming for blood and firing their muskets.

Gunner's crew grew tense. They craned over the rails, hands twitching at their swords, ready for their part in the battle. With only seconds to go before they were rammed by the death-giver, Gunner ordered a brilliant manoeuvre. "Back the topsails!" he yelled. *The Dandylion's* masts shuddered under the move and the ship slowed dramatically.

The Revenge, not anticipating *The Dandylion's* sudden drop in speed, swooped past, missing them by centimetres. Now Gunner had the advantage. "Fire!" he ordered and, with a deafening roar, *The Dandylion's* cannonballs skimmed across *The Revenge*'s decks, sending several men flying. In the bowels of the ship, the shuddering explosion from the cannons split the air, choking Jack and Mahoot with acrid smoke. Up above, Gunner's crew fired their muskets for good measure.

Blacktooth, realising that his opportunity to destroy *The Dandylion* was lost, tacked to port to chase after Snotty, who was attempting to break away. He quickly overhauled the slower boat, running to her port-side and angling his death-giver so he could rip *The Tormenter* open.

Snotty, just ahead, took her chance to avoid the death-giver by tacking across Blacktooth's bow. A sudden wind shift blew her off course and her rigging caught in *The Revenge*'s bowsprit. The breeze brought her crashing around. Blacktooth's metal spikes caught at her hull and stabbed into the

timber, grinding and tearing a huge hole just
above the water line.

Seeing Blacktooth caught fast against
Snotty's boat, Gunner moved to attack from
the starboard side. As Snotty and Blacktooth's
crew fired their muskets at point-blank range,
Gunner fired his cannons.

Blacktooth fired back at *The Dandylion*
immediately and, as Al ran with shot to
the sailors, a cannonball whistled past his
ears, cutting the topside halyard away and
threatening to send the foretop crashing to

the deck. Another cannonball blew a hole
below decks, the impact shuddering through
Al's feet. Then another cannonball roared
through the bulkheads, sending a shower
of splinters through the air. A barb caught
Mahoot's arm, tumbling him backwards.
Jack, his ears ringing, found blood running
down his face. Some men fell, groaning,
while others drew back, blood-spattered.
The uninjured regrouped and bravely
awaited orders from above.

Gunner closed in on Blacktooth, ordering
the muskets to fire, and soon the pirate crews
were firing through a haze of smoke and
confusion. Mozzy, seeing the rigging failing
fast, clambered into the ratlines to repair the
halyard. For several tense minutes, with shots
whistling around his head, he worked in the
swaying rigging, eventually fixing the line
and sliding safely back to deck.

Blacktooth, realising he was now trapped

between two boats, wrenched at the helm
and pulled *The Revenge* free of *The Tormenter*,
leaving Gunner with the sun in his face,
and The Revenge bearing down on him,
all guns firing.

"Give no quarter!" screamed Blacktooth
from the poop deck, as he positioned his
attack in such a way that the death-giver
would slice *The Dandylion* in half within
minutes.

Al realised that Gunner needed to buy
several precious seconds so he could tack
his ship, without Blacktooth seeing the
manoeuvre and changing his course, too.
With only seconds before the boats
collided, Al raced to Gunner's cabin,
grabbed a shaving mirror and tore back
to the poop deck. Standing with his
legs spread apart to stop himself from
flying sideways, Al caught the sun and
aimed the glare from the looking-glass

straight at Blacktooth's murderous face.

The unexpected bolt of sunlight temporarily blinded the pirate, and the boats shaved past each other, the death-giver only glancing off *The Dandylion*'s hull.

Once again Gunner had the advantage. He aimed a broadside cannon blast at Blacktooth. The balls rocketed through the air, one catching the portside death-giver and blowing it to smithereens. Shards of metal spiralled into the air and a hole gaped in *The Revenge*'s hull. The weight of the heavy starboard death-giver dragged the ship sideways, pulling the sails towards the ocean.

A great cheer erupted from *The Dandylion* as the ruined ship slowly rolled on its beam, taking water fast. Some of Blacktooth's men fell into the heaving ocean and, as Al looked down into the darkening seas, a green fin cut the water. "Greeny Joe!" he cried in horror, as the giant shark went to hunt his

supper. He looked across the horizon to see
Blacktooth's pirates lowering their longboats
and rowing away from their sinking ship.

With Blacktooth's boat in its death roll,
Gunner broke away to port and sailed
onwards. Snotty tacked to starboard and,
despite the crippled state of *The Tormenter*,
fired a parting shot at *The Dandylion* as she
fled towards the horizon.

The Elephant Statue

Safely anchored at Sabre Island, Gunner set
about repairing the damage to *The Dandylion*.
The boys went straight to Mahoot's
grandfather, who bandaged Mahoot's arm
and cleaned Jack's forehead. Then they took
more bandages down to the beach and, with
the boys' help, Mahoot's grandfather set a
broken arm, cleaned wounds and stitched
gashes in arms and legs.

"No painkillers or anaesthetics," said Al in awe, watching the wounded pirates grit their teeth as the old man's needle and thread tied their gaping wounds neatly together.

"I know," said Jack. "How do they cope?"

The following day, Gunner's crew went to Alleric Castle early to search for the elephant statue. They arrived to discover Vampire Zu, Snotty's first mate, leaning out of an upstairs window. He was dangling a man by his feet, and the man was hammering at an elephant gargoyle on the castle walls, hoping to find the map in the carved waterspout.

"Shiver me timbers and buckets of blood! Snotty's already here," cursed Gunner, taking aim with his musket. A bullet whizzed past Vampire's head, causing him to let out a mighty howl and pull the dangling sailor back inside.

Within seconds Snotty Nell arrived at

the castle gates
with a crew of
armed men.
"Be prepared to
die," she snarled,
brandishing a
sword in one hand
while her pirates ran
at them, screaming.

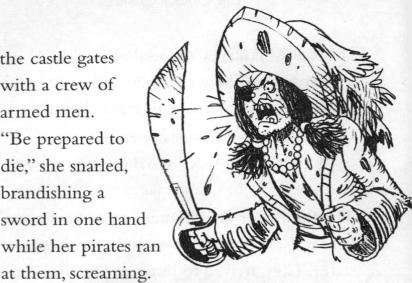

For several minutes the pirates battled,
but Gunner's crew was outnumbered and,
realising they would not get into the castle
without loss of life, Gunner ordered the men
into the jungle.

"Chicken-livered weakling!" screamed
Snotty as slime dribbled from her nose.
"This treasure's mine!"

"How long have you been searching,
you incompetent nincompoop?" Gunner
yelled back.

"I'll find it," bragged Snotty, "and then I'll

come after you, you gutless wonder!"

Gunner smiled at her words. "So she hasn't found it yet," he said to his crew. "We're gunner wait and watch. If she finds it we'll follow her." He turned to Mozzy. "Stay here and keep watch. Come and get us if she sets sail. She has a big hole in her boat, so she won't get anywhere too fast."

That night, while everyone was sitting around a fire outside Mahoot's grandfather's house, Mozzy returned. "It's too dark to search anymore," he said, "and Snotty's made camp on the beach. Some of her men are pulling a big canvas sail over the hole in her boat. She's not going anywhere for now and I don't think they've found anything."

Snakeboot uncurled himself from a warm spot near the fire, stretched and walked towards Al. He lifted a front paw, touched Al's leg and meowed.

"Snakeboot can see in the dark," said Al. "How about if Jack, Mahoot and I take him to the castle?"

"As I've said many times before," replied Gunner, "that cat and you boys are lucky. Off you go, but don't be too long. I don't want to lose sleep waiting up for you."

Al, Jack and Mahoot lit torches and made their way to Alleric Castle, which glimmered in the moonlight. As they walked through the entrance hall, their feet crunched on the crumbled carvings left behind by Snotty's ransacking pirates.

Snakeboot led the boys through corridors, up winding stairs and into several large moonlit rooms in the upper storeys.

"I guess these were once bedrooms," said Al, admiring the low-relief engravings on the doorways and walls.

"There aren't any statues here, though," said Jack.

"What we need to find," said Mahoot, "is something that my ring can fit into." He held up his elephant-head ring, with its curling trunk and tusks thrusting outwards. "If my ring works like Jack's did on Ruby Island then it should fit into a carving on a wall. There are hundreds of them all over the castle."

"But not many elephants, luckily," said Jack. "More antelopes, giraffes and loads of sea creatures."

"Sea creatures!" exclaimed Al. "You've just given me an idea." He ran to a wall and began to inspect it. "We have to search for Halimeda's bedroom," he explained. "Remember what Prince Alleric said to Halimeda: I've put it inside your elephant. He didn't say elephant statue. Only the butler said that he thought it was a statue."

"But how on earth will we figure out which one was Halimeda's bedroom?" asked

Mahoot. "There are so many rooms here."

"The clue is in her name." said Al. "I looked it up. It means fascinated by the sea, and you just said there are walls here covered in sea creatures."

"We passed through a room like that a bit further back. It was full of marine life pictures," said Mahoot.

The boys ran back down the hall and entered a spacious room, overlooking the ocean. The lights from Snotty's fires on the foreshore gleamed through the trees.

"I think we should put our torches out," warned Jack. "We don't want to attract attention. We can explore in the moonlight."

As he spoke, a strange sound stopped them. They listened in silence for a few seconds. "Probably a rat or something," said Al, dismissing it. "Let's start looking for that elephant."

Carefully, the boys checked over the

highly decorated walls. Whales and dolphins, flying fish and octopuses and, finally, a small line of elephants looped over a small doorway that led to a bathroom. Mahoot explored each beast with his fingers until he found one with three holes in its body. Carefully he lifted his ring and pressed it against the carving. There was a loud click and a cupboard door opened in the wall.

Inside, in a finely carved drawer, was an aged parchment.

Al looked over Mahoot's shoulder to get a closer look.

"Well done! We've found the map!" he cried. "Snotty will waste days looking for this, and by the time she realises it's been taken, we'll be long gone."

Mahoot grinned in agreement, pocketed the map and together they left the castle.

Unknown to the boys, they had not been the only ones in the castle. Grenda, Snotty Nell's daughter, had been bored and had returned to the ruins to do some exploring of her own. Recognising the boys, she had ducked into the darkest shadows and then carefully followed them. Although she didn't see them pocket the map, she heard every word, and as soon as they left Alleric Castle she ran as fast as she could back to her mother.

Hidden Treasure

Several days later, under stormy skies, the boys found themselves standing in the centre of a long-abandoned town. Gunner consulted the treasure map and looked up. "Well, we're here at the town centre, but what now?"

"Four o'clock. Tick-tock," Al read from the map. A ruined clock tower cast a shadow across the town square. "There's the clock tower, but the clock's missing. Should we go inside and take a look?"

"Ding, dong, dell," read Jack, peering over Al's shoulder. "There's no bell in the tower either."

"The sun's over the yardarm," said Gunner, "but how do we tell when it's exactly four o'clock without going back to the boat?"

"Hasn't anyone got a watch?" asked Jack.

"We don't need anyone on watch," answered Mozzy. "Snotty's still back on Sabre Island and she's got no idea where we are."

"I mean, hasn't anyone got a clock on their wrist?" said Jack, remembering that he was in a time when watches had not yet been invented.

"Are you mad?" said Slicer, the cook. "You just try lifting the clock on board ship."

"So, should we be looking for a clock or a bell?" asked Gunner.

Al cast his eyes around the town centre once again as a cloud passed over the sun, obliterating the clock tower's shadow.

"Ding, dong, dell," sang Mahoot. "Where is the bell?"

"Ding, dong, dell, pussy's in the well," sang Jack, tickling Snakeboot's ears.

As Jack sang his rhyme, Al spotted a brick-walled well with a bucket and rope hanging from a scaffold at one end of the town square. Despite the gathering stormclouds above, the clock tower's shadow would eventually travel towards the well. "The treasure's down the well!" cried Al.

Mahoot was lowered on the rope to the bottom of the well until he stood in waist-deep water. "I'll feel around with my feet and see if I can find anything!" he called up. After a few seconds of splashing about he gave a cry of victory, then ducked under the water and brought up a casket.

"We've got it!" cried Gunner.

"No, we've got it!" screeched a woman's

voice from behind them. Gunner turned
to find Snotty and her crew, armed with
muskets. "Hands up, you weevils," she
ordered. "Throw down your weapons or
we'll shoot you where you stand."

While Snotty's crew gathered their
weapons, Snotty marched over to the well
and pushed Gunner to one side, peering
down. "You, boy!" she yelled at Mahoot.
"Show us what you've found!"

Mahoot, seeing Snotty's face, dropped the
casket with a splash. As Snotty leaned over the
side of the well, trying to see what the boy had
dropped, the old wall of the well crumbled
inwards and Snotty, already off balance, fell
with a scream and a frightening splash.

"Are you all right?" Vampire Zu called
down the well.

"*I* am," Mahoot called back. "She just
missed me."

"Not you!" Vampire snapped. "Captain

Nell, are you all right?"

"She's underwater and I can't pull her up," yelled Mahoot.

"Mum!" screamed Grenda, who had run over from a building at the edge of the town square. "Mum! Are you all right?"

"I can't get her head above water!" yelled Mahoot. "I think she's drowning!"

"Save her!" Grenda pleaded, turning to Vampire Zu. "Do something, quickly."

Vampire Zu looked down the well. "I'm too big to go down," he said. "I'd get stuck."

"I'll go," offered Gunner, patting the girl's shoulder. "Don't worry, Grenda." He grabbed the rope from Vampire Zu and lowered himself down.

"She's not moving," came Gunner's voice several seconds later. "Send down another rope and we'll haul her out."

Gunner and Mahoot worked together to lift Snotty back to the surface, where

she lay lifeless on the ground. Grenda
sat beside her, weeping. Vampire Zu bent
down, putting his face near Snotty's mouth.

"Can't feel any breath," he said, hoisting
her up to show everyone her still features.

Vampire Zu stood up, stared arrogantly at the assembled pirates and announced, "Snotty's dead. I'm the boss now."

Grenda let out a wail of terror and grief. "No!" she cried, flinging herself across her mother's body.

Vampire Zu turned to Mahoot with an evil stare. "Get back down and get that treasure. And be quick about it, or I'll shoot your captain."

Scared, Mahoot clambered back down the well, while Grenda sobbed inconsolably. Al moved to her side and patted her shoulder. "We'll try to save your mum," he tried to reassure her.

"How?" she wept. "She's dead. Dead is dead."

"Any of you know resuscitation?" Al asked the pirates who stood nearby.

His question was met with bewilderment, so he tried again. "You know, the kiss of life?

Do any of you know the kiss of life to help Snotty?"

"Kiss of life?" one of the pirates chortled. "Never heard of that one. Giving Snotty a kiss would probably kill us."

"There's a resuscitation picture at my local pool," said Jack. "If I tell you what I remember, could you try to do it?"

Al nodded. "It's worth a shot," he said.

"You're not shooting her too," laughed another pirate.

"First, clear the airways," said Jack, ignoring the men standing around them. "I think you have to use your fingers."

"Errrk," cried the pirates, as Al pulled a big booger from Snotty's scarred nose and peered down her throat.

"All clear," said Al.

"Then tip her head back, hold her nostrils and breathe into her mouth," continued Jack.

Al shut his eyes, put his lips to Snotty's

blue, cold mouth and breathed. Nothing
happened.

"Look, the kid's kissin' Snotty," said one of
the pirates. "How revoltin'."

Al bravely tried again. This time, as he
breathed, Snotty's chest moved, her eyes
fluttered, and she groaned and wheezed. Al
stumbled backwards as she sat up and vomited.

A gasp of surprise came from the pirates.
Vampire Zu looked upset. Mahoot emerged
from the well carrying the golden casket, a
flash of lightning at that moment highlighting
the radiance of the gold.

If Snotty had any ill effects from her
near-death experience they were quickly
dispersed at the sight of the treasure.
"Beautiful booty," she puffed and, still
struggling for air, staggered to her feet and
snatched the prize from Mahoot's grasp.

As a roll of thunder shuddered around them,
Snotty turned to Vampire Zu and said, "Throw

The Dandylion's crew down the well!"

"Mum!" shouted Grenda. "Al just saved your life."

"Oh," said Snotty in surprise, "did he?"

"That kid gave you a big kiss while you were unconscious," said Vampire Zu, pointing at Al.

"Yuck," replied Snotty, wiping her mouth. "Perhaps I should shoot him."

"No!" Grenda insisted. "He helped you to breathe. Vampire Zu said you were dead, but Al saved you."

"Hhmm, if you say so," said Snotty.
"I won't throw them down the well, then."
She glared at her pirate crew, considering
her next move. "Get ropes and tie them up
— along with Vampire Zu, and take a few
men and heave *The Dandylion*'s cannons
overboard. Make sure they don't have *any*
weapons." Another flash of lightning lit
the sky and the wind picked up. "There's
a big storm brewing and we're on a bad
anchorage," said Snotty. "We'll have to move
quickly. We need to lash another sail over
the hole on *The Tormenter* before we weigh
anchor and head back to town."

Thunderstorms and Whirlwinds

Just as Snotty was leaving with the casket of sapphires, Grenda sneaked over to Al and slipped a pocket knife between his fingers. "Thank you," she whispered, before running after her mother.

Grenda's act of kindness meant it wasn't long before Al cut himself free and then released the rest of the crew. But when they got back to *The Dandylion*, Snotty had already set sail. They set about fixing the damage Vampire Zu had created on board. As they worked, repairing cut ropes and broken rails, lightning flashed across the sky.

Order restored, Gunner finally pulled anchor and *The Dandylion* raced through the heaving swells, her prow buried in white water, rain lashing down and pouring from the sails.

"This storm is the worst I've seen in years," shouted Gunner, as a massive lightning clap turned the world upside down.

Suddenly, a cloud of blue light shimmered around the crow's nest. It hovered, ghost-like, for several seconds, then separated into glowing balls that rolled down the rigging before exploding over the ocean in a fiery display.

"What on earth was that?" Al gasped in surprise.

"Ball lightning," replied Gunner. "You get

it at sea sometimes. It will chase you if you're wearing weapons — it's attracted to metal. It can kill a man if it hits him. We could've lost the boat if we were carrying cannons."

Another massive clap of thunder split the air, and Gunner laughed heartily with relief. "That silly old trout may have just saved our lives by chucking our cannons overboard."

A short while later Gunner lifted the telescope to his eyes. "It's *The Tormenter*," he said, "and it's wallowing like a harpooned whale."

Gunner ordered *The Dandylion* hard to starboard, and they plunged through the heaving swells until the enemy ship was clearly visible.

Ball lightning flickered around its decks,
highlighting the damage it had caused.
Cannons hung from gaping wounds in
the hull and the sail that had been used
to repair the hole lay in shreds. Water was
pouring into the belly of the ship, making
it list dangerously. Snotty and some of the
crew were trying to lower longboats, but
they bucked and swayed against the gigantic
waves, unable to launch.

Gunner headed into the wind, his sails flapping thunderously. "I'm gunner enjoy watching this," he said.

As soon as Snotty, Grenda, Vampire and some of the crew clambered into one of the lifeboats, Gunner saw the casket of sapphires and made his move. He brought *The Dandylion* up beside his old enemy. "You have two choices!" he screamed into the wind. "Climb aboard and we'll save you, or stay

where you are and we'll run you down!"

Another massive blast of lightning split the air as Snotty yelled something and made a very rude sign.

In answer, *The Dandylion* bore down on the tiny lifeboat wallowing helplessly before them.

Within seconds of a collision, Snotty waved a white handkerchief. "I give up!" she screamed.

"Hooray!" cried Gunner. "The treasure's mine!"

As Gunner got ready to sail away, with Snotty, Grenda and the casket of sapphires safely on board, there was a sudden quietening of the wind. The swell turned to a chop and a peculiar silence hung over the ocean. The dark storm clouds became darker and everyone looked around fearfully. Suddenly Grenda pointed.

"WATERSPOUT!" screamed several pirates at once. One hundred metres away a giant

worm of blackness curled towards
The Dandylion.

To Al's horror, the sea reared up and
the beast was upon them. There was a
tremendous roar as the sails were wrenched
from the masts and the boat spun wildly,
knocking everyone to the decks.

The air streamed upwards with a scream,
sucking the breath from Al's body and lifting
The Dandylion from the water. Hurled off his
feet and twirled through the air like a feather
in a vacuum cleaner, Al managed to grab at
a rope that flew before him in the whirling
destruction. Using every muscle in his body
to fight the force of the wind, he clung to
the rigging for his life, before the spout
finally released him. *The Dandylion* quivered
from end to end and shuddered back into the
boiling cauldron of white water below.

Screaming, Al was pitched downwards
into the sea, dragged by the rope that had

just saved his life. He let go and, kicking
with all his remaining strength, surfaced.
The upturned hull of *The Dandylion* floated
nearby, and he managed to thrash his way
to it, hauling himself from the churning
sea. Clambering up he found Gunner and
Snotty already sitting side by side, each
gripping the golden treasure casket with
vicious determination. Jack was also in the
water nearby, grimly holding Grenda above
the waves. Al clambered back down the hull
to pull them both on board, just as Mahoot
swam towards them, ashen-faced but alive.

Mozzy was hanging onto the boom with
Slicer and Vampire Zu. Sharkbait, Snotty's
bosun, was collected from a mangled cabin
door. Eventually some thirty people, and a
bedraggled Snakeboot, sat on *The Dandylion*'s
hull as the storm clouds cleared. They were
lucky to be alive.

Shipwrecked

A slow current moved *The Dandylion*'s hulk through the sea as the sun beat down, baking Al's head, drying his tongue and blistering his skin. The barnacles on the wooden hull made his bottom sore, but he didn't dare try to get into the water to cool down, having seen Greeny Joe circling.

"There's no sail, no shelter, no water and no food. This is pretty bad," moaned Vampire Zu as he gazed into the brilliant waters.

It was even worse when night fell.

There was no space to sleep, for if anyone tried to lie down it made less room for everyone else. Neither Gunner nor Snotty moved from their position in the centre of the boat, glaring at each other with hatred, the casket between them.

"Chuck it away," growled a pirate. "We can't eat sapphires and they're taking up space."

"I'm not giving up," said Gunner, glaring at Snotty. "This is mine by rights."

"I'm waiting for you to fall asleep and fall overboard," Snotty sneered.

The stalemate continued.

The following day, Al's throat was as dry as a sandpit. He looked across at Jack, whose lips were cracked and bleeding. "I'm so thirsty," he croaked. "And we're surrounded by water."

"Don't ever drink sea water," warned

Mahoot. "It'll make you go mad."

But as the hours went by, Al couldn't help but wonder how the cool water that lapped at his feet would taste. Just one sip, he thought, and he bent towards the tempting blue.

"That's my water," growled one of Snotty's pirates, pushing Al savagely in the back. Al would have fallen but for Jack, who grabbed him and pulled him back. Still Greeny Joe circled nearby, watching the drama.

The pirate glared at Al with frantic, red-ringed eyes and, already driven mad by thirst, bent over and drank greedily from the sea.

"You stupid fool!" shouted Vampire Zu, seizing the pirate and forcing him away from the water. The pirate struggled against Vampire Zu with surprising strength. When he was finally subdued, everyone sat back and a heavy silence descended.

The sun beat down and Al began to dream of his kitchen tap at home and all the glasses in the cupboards brimming with water.

"How long do you think we can last?" whispered Mahoot.

"If we're not murdered first, no more than three days without water," replied Jack.

Just as the afternoon sun sunk lower, Al noticed something on the horizon. He squinted into the glare. "Look," he said, nudging Jack. "Is that an island?"

The pirate who drank the sea water overheard. He too squinted into the sun. "There's an island!" he yelled.

Everyone turned. "No," said Gunner, "it's a mirage. Look, it's upside down."

Sure enough, to Al's disappointment, the island appeared the wrong way up and shimmered oddly, to prove it wasn't real.

"Liar!" screamed the pirate at Captain Gunner. "You're going to let us die here." He stood up. "I'm leaving," he cried. "Anyone who tries to stop me is a dead man!"

"You'll be dead yourself, you lunatic," said Snotty. "You can't swim for starters, there's a shark in the ocean, and you're not in your right mind from the sea water you've been drinking." She glared at him. "Just shut up and sit down!"

The pirate obeyed but muttered angrily under his breath. "I'll kill you all."

The day wore on and despite Al's best

intentions to stay awake and watch the
murderous pirate, he failed. When he opened
his eyes it was dark. Looking about him, he
saw that Jack was asleep, leaning on Mahoot,
who in turn was asleep leaning on Grenda,
who had her head on her mother's lap.
Snotty's head was drooping over the casket
and so was Gunner's. The pirate who had
drunk the sea water was nowhere to be seen.

Al shuddered in horror.

The Competition

Just before dawn Snakeboot jumped into Al's lap, waking him from another slumber. Al licked his parched lips and patted the cat. "It's all right for you, Snakeboot," he sighed. "You're magical and can't die. You might have led us to more of Prince Alleric's treasure, but it won't do us any good if we don't have water. You should have let me sleep."

Suddenly the grinding of rocks on wood alerted Al to the reason Snakeboot had woken him. *The Dandylion* was lifting in the swell and coming down on land. Out of the gloom, the broken mast of a ship and the cry of disturbed sea birds confirmed they were ashore. Snakeboot purred and his purple eyes gleamed in satisfaction as Al shouted and woke everyone from their troubled sleep.

Shipwreck Island appeared with the sun's first rays, and there was a rush to wade ashore in search of fresh water. Gunner and Snotty, still attached to their treasure chest, were soon issuing orders to find stores on the wrecked ships around them. Stale and mouldy as some of the supplies were, they were shared out and before long everyone felt better.

Because neither Snotty nor Gunner would relinquish their hold on the golden casket, both pirate crews gathered around their captains and stared aggressively at each other.

"One of 'em will fall asleep soon,"

growled one pirate, "and then we'll grab the
casket and attack."

When Al could stand it no longer, he went
over to Gunner and Snotty with an idea he
hoped would break the deadlock. "Why don't
you have a competition to decide who'll own
the casket?" he suggested.

"That's a good idea," said Gunner. "How
about it, Nell? What if we put the treasure
down, and our crews work together to build a
raft and find some weapons. When that's done,
we captains will fight each other. Winner
takes all: the raft and the sapphires."

Snotty smiled and her one eye glinted with malice. She spat on her hand. "It's a deal," she said, confident she would win.

"The loser will have to make another raft after the winner leaves," Gunner added, before he too spat on his hand and held it out.

The wrecked boats were duly raided for wood, ropes and sails and, two days later, a fine raft with a small sail stood ready on the beach. Several swords had also been discovered and the weapons lay beside the sapphires.

"As I'm a gentleman, I'll let you have first choice," said Gunner. "Pick one."

Snotty chose a fine-bladed, two-edged sword and lifted it defiantly. "To the death," Snotty cried, cutting the air with a swish. Her pirates cheered.

Gunner picked a light, somewhat rusty rapier and stepped forward. With blades flashing, Snotty and Gunner began their duel.

Slowly but surely Snotty forced Gunner backwards. "She's amazing," whispered Jack in awe, "and she's only got one eye."

"I can't believe Gunner's so useless," said Al as Snotty cut at Gunner's coat. Gunner turned at the strike, running backwards towards the rocks at the end of the beach, before facing his foe again.

"Coward!" Snotty screamed. "I always said you were weaker than dishwater!" She swiped at Gunner again and he retreated further.

"Slit his gizzards!" yelled Vampire Zu, as the rest of Snotty's crew urged her on.

"Perhaps he's a bit soft on Snotty still," said Jack. "I've never seen him look so weak before."

"I don't think he wants to kill her," said Al. "And we don't want him killed. Perhaps he's got some sort of plan where they'll both end up all right."

Snotty pressed her advantage until Gunner was stumbling over rocks on a narrow reef that ran out into the ocean. Waves churned in the deep currents running on either side as Gunner rock-hopped backwards towards the sea.

The pirates followed, barracking and cat-calling, enthralled by their battle. "There's no hope for him once he gets to the last rock," Vampire Zu chortled. "Old Snotty's got him boxed in. Soon the sapphires will be ours."

But the rocks on the reef were slimy and Snotty kept slipping. A green fin cut the water beside her and circled. Snotty stopped, her eye wild with fear at the sight of the shark. Gunner, with a smug smile, lunged at her with his rapier. His plan was working.

Snotty tripped, her sword flew from her
grasp and, arms flailing, she teetered on
the edge of the reef. Finally, she overbalanced
and Greeny Joe opened his massive jaws
in anticipation.

Gunner, quick as a wink,
leapt forward and grabbed
Snotty around the waist,
saving her from certain
death. "You'll say I've
won, fair and square,"
he threatened, "or
I'm gunner let
go and..."

"Not Greeny Joe!" Snotty wailed. "I'd rather be sliced in half than let that monster eat me!"

"So, do I win?" Gunner asked.

"He's won!" Snotty called. "Fair and square, Gunner's won!"

Seaworthy Again

Gunner swaggered up and down the docks, admiring various ships that were for sale. "None of them does the trick for me, so far," he said. "Most of my treasure went down with *The Dandylion*; I need a boat that'll keep my treasure safe."

Eventually, in the dry dock, he spied a nimble three-masted sloop that had just been built and was being painted. "I'll bet she's faster than anything I've seen *and* can carry a few cannons," he said admiringly. Without waiting to find out if she was for sale or not, he hunted down her owner and offered a price in sapphires that couldn't be refused.

Thrilled with his new property, Gunner immediately set to fitting her out in a grand manner. He ordered new sails, had her hull reinforced with copper and his cabin painted in gold leaf. "This boat will gleam like sunlight and strike fear into all who see her," he boasted. "She'll be just about invincible. Like you, Al, when you wear your scabbard." He patted the ship's main mast. "In fact, I'm gunner call her *The Invincible*, and I'll have the Dragon Blood Sabre painted on her hull for luck."

Meanwhile, Snotty Nell was making her way into port on a raft, somewhat the worse for wear. A few days later Gunner heard she had already managed to buy a ship. "I think we'll take a walk down the docks and see what she's got," said Gunner. "I can't imagine how she got a boat this quickly. She must've sold her soul to Spong and gone into debt."

Gunner soon sighted Snotty on the bridge of a worn-out Indiaman with patched sails and a stained, unpainted hull.

The old boat was broad in the beam and heavy in the water.

"She'd be mighty uncomfortable in a swell," Gunner told the boys. "I'd hate to be on board that ship in a storm." As he came closer, his eyes lit up with merriment as the name, *Nausi VIII*, became visible on the prow.

"You'll wallow like a stupid old pig!" Gunner roared from the quay. "A stupid pig on a fat, ugly, slow boat!"

Snotty shook her fist at him and yelled back, "You're the stupid old pig!"

"Stupid, am I?" shouted Gunner. "I'm the one with all the sapphires!"

"Don't think you got them all," Snotty sniggered. "I grabbed a few handfuls while you were sleeping. You didn't even miss them!"

"Blistering barnacles!" hissed Gunner under his breath. "I should've counted them. That wicked old weevil's always coming up trumps."

Later, back on *The Invincible*, Gunner had a surprise for the boys. He called them down below decks and led them to a small cabin. "I've had this fixed up just for you," he said. "You boys deserve a promotion. You are now officially my midshipmen." He pointed to a small velvet cushion. "I've even given Snakeboot some recognition," he smiled.

Snakeboot purred loudly, jumped onto the plump cushion and made himself comfortable.

"Now, we're all set," Gunner added, "and we'll sail by the end of the week. There's loads of treasure still to be found, and we're gunner be the ones to get it all. I feel quite invincible."

"Speaking of being invincible," Al said to Jack later, as they lay in their hammocks in their new cabin, "I'd still like to try and find

another dragon diamond for the scabbard."

"I think they'll be difficult to find,"
said Jack. "There aren't any clues to their
whereabouts. Vicious Victor gave them to
his horrible friends, but no one knows
who they are."

"But if they still have the diamonds they'll
be deathless like Razor Toe," said Al. "Someone,
somewhere, must know who they are."

Jack reached out and patted Snakeboot, who was sleeping on his new cushion beside the boys. "Are you going to take us home, Snakeboot, or are you going to help us find another black diamond before we return?"

The cat blinked twice and his strange purple eyes glowed with adventurous intensity.

"I'm sure that means we're staying here for a while," said Jack. "But where should we start looking? Snakeboot can't talk to tell us where to go."

"There could be more clues about the scabbard and the sabre in Alleric Castle," said Al. "Or maybe a hint about the rings that Vicious Victor gave Hally and me. I'm sure they were stolen from Alleric Castle."

Snakeboot flicked his ears, stood, arched his back, then leapt from his cushion and ran to the cabin door.

"That looks like an answer," said Al.

"I think he wants us to go back to Sabre Island."

"Let's ask Gunner," suggested Jack as he climbed out of his hammock. "He doesn't have a course planned, and I'm sure he'll take us to the island if we tell him there's more treasure to be found..."

Captain's Code

Can you decipher the following message
written in multiplication code? Check out
www.dragonbloodpirates.co.uk for the keys
to Captain's Code...if you dare!

42,7,45,9,18

36,50,45

14,36,35

45,18,11

60,36,28,8,24,11,40

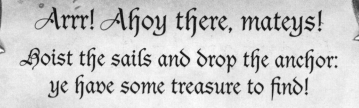

Arrr! Ahoy there, mateys!
Hoist the sails and drop the anchor: ye have some treasure to find!

One swashbucklin' reader will win an ipod Touch and ten runners up will win a Dragon Blood Pirates booty bag. For a chance to win, ye must dare to unearth the treasure!

Each of the six Dragon Blood Pirates: **The Legend of Dragon Island** books contain a clue.
When you have solved the six clues, enter the answers online at www.dragonbloodpirates.co.uk

Or send your name, address and answers to:

Dragon Blood Pirates:
The Legend of Dragon Island
338 Euston Road, London NW1 3BH

Best o' luck, me hearties!

To find where the pirate treasure lies,
ye must find the answer to the clue that lies below:

A bitter battle sunk this dreadful ship,
Then from a shark its crew did get a nip.

Only one entry per child. Final draw 31 August 2011.
For full terms and conditions visit
www.dragonbloodpirates.co.uk/terms

www.dragonbloodpirates.co.uk

Ahoy there shipmates!

To reel in amazin' pirate booty, steer smartly
towards www.dragonbloodpirates.co.uk

Ye'll find games, downloads, activities and
sneak previews of the latest swashbucklin'
Dragon Blood Pirates adventures.
Learn how to speak all pirate-like, how to find
out what type of pirate ye be, an' what pirate
games ye can play with yer mates! This treasure
trove is a sure feast fer yer deadlights!

Only the bravest an' heartiest amon' ye
can become a true scurvy dog, so don't
ye miss a thing and sign up to yer newsletter
at www.dragonbloodpirates.co.uk!

Don't ye miss book nine in the

Dragon Blood Pirates

series!

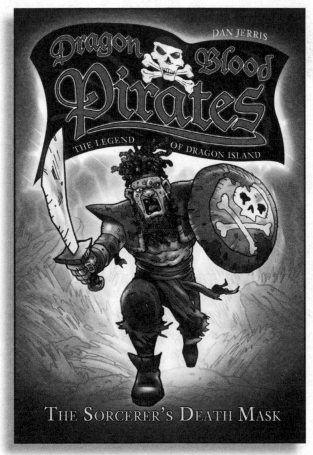

Turn the page and shiver yer timbers
with a slice of the next high-seas adventure...

The Missing Diamonds

Al Breas and his best friend Jack Seabrook were sailing through the Dragon Blood Islands on *The Invincible*, with Captain Gunner at the helm. Al peered through the morning mists as Sabre Island came into view. His heart raced at the idea of exploring Alleric Castle once again. There were so many secrets in the ruins.

"We're gunner drop anchor by

mid-morning," said Captain Gunner. He glanced down at Al's waist. "Though I must say I'm a bit worried about where you hid your sabre and scabbard. You don't want someone nasty stealing them."

"They won't," said Al confidently. "They're somewhere very safe."

"Nothing's safe around here," said Gunner. "It might be better if you gave them to me. Perhaps you should tell me where they are."

Al shook his head. "Sorry, Gunner, but I can't tell you. I don't think the scabbard's safe to wear, which is why I've hidden it. Even though we've found one of the missing black diamonds, we have to find all four before the scabbard will work properly and make its wearer invincible. One black diamond on its own is a terrible thing. It makes its owner deathless."

Years earlier, an evil pirate named Vicious Victor had stolen the Scabbard of

Invincibility from its owner, Prince Alleric, and, not realising the immense powers of its black dragon diamonds, had ripped them from the scabbard and given them to four of his pirate friends. Al and Jack had since found the scabbard, as well as the Dragon Blood Sabre, but were now trying to restore their powers by locating the missing black diamonds.

Gunner shrugged, disappointed at Al's answer. "Well, you can trust me," he said. "I'm not gunner get nasty, but I wouldn't mind being deathless. Are you sure you won't tell me?"

Al was tempted to laugh. The sabre and scabbard were hidden in Al's house: in number five Drake Drive, back in the twenty-first century. Gunner would never understand that Al and Jack had arrived in the Dragon Blood Islands by stepping into a magical sea trunk that had once belonged to

Al's grandfather and which now sat in
Al's attic.

Al's thoughts were interrupted by
the arrival of his friend Mahoot, who
clambered up on deck, carrying a
three-legged white cat.

"Snakeboot's getting lazy," said Mahoot.

"He was just sitting on the cushion in the cabin, purring. He needs some action."

"Like helping us find more treasure?" said Captain Gunner hopefully.

The Sorcerer of Dragon Island

The following day everyone on *The Invincible* searched Alleric Castle for signs of hidden treasure. As the hours wore on, Gunner and his crew gave up and returned to the ship. The boys were not so easily discouraged and continued exploring, following Snakeboot as he wandered from room to room.

Eventually, Snakeboot went into an empty hallway and sat by a window.

"I give up," said Mahoot, looking around. "There's nothing here."

"Come on, Snakeboot," Jack urged. "Show us something."

Snakeboot purred. "If Snakeboot's sitting down, it could be a clue," said Al. "We should look at the wall paintings again, like we did last time we were here."

"And look for another keyhole where my elephant ring might fit," said Mahoot. "We know Prince Alleric used my ring as a key to secret cupboards and things."

"Good idea," said Jack. "Last time it was in an elephant painting. Let's look at the elephants painted on the walls."

"I wonder what *my* ring is for," said Al, looking at the ruby-eyed dragon ring he wore on his thumb. "Maybe it's a key, too."

It didn't take the boys long to find a painted elephant with three tiny holes in its body. Excitedly, Mahoot pressed his elephant ring into each of the holes in turn. It worked! Soon there was a loud click and the slow grinding of wheels, then the wall swung inwards, revealing a secret study, filled with books.

On a table, covered in years' worth of dust, a book lay open as if it had been left half-read.

"This might be worth a look," said Al. He sat at the table and turned to the book's cover. It was called *The History of the Sabre*. "Check this out," he said. "There's heaps in here about the making of the Dragon Blood Sabre and the Scabbard of Invincibility."

Mahoot and Jack peered over Al's shoulder as he turned the brittle pages. "According to this, the prince of Alleric Castle back then had the sabre and its scabbard forged by a magician who lived on an island of dragons." Al pointed to a drawing of the magician in the book. "This sorcerer first made the sabre and gave the prince some magical words so it would take him through space and time." Al turned a few more pages before he continued the story. "But when the sorcerer made the scabbard he took four scales from a dragon and, with a magical forge, created four black diamonds. Then further on it says, '… The great prince paid a king's fortune for his magical weapon and, pleased with his treasures, he decided to order more wonders from the sorcerer on Dragon Island. He returned a year later to collect two magical rings: a dragon with ruby eyes for his son, and a pearl one for his daughter…'"

"They must be the rings Vicious Victor gave you and your sister," said Mahoot. "Isn't that strange?"

"It sure is," said Al, looking at his ring with new interest.

"Read on," urged Jack.

Al turned back to the pages. "'...While the prince was on the island, the sorcerer died. Amidst much wailing and grief, his body was buried in a golden coffin, clothed in silver, and a golden death mask set upon his face. His powers while he was alive were so immense that everyone feared him even in death, and no one dared touch his vast treasure. They buried everything with him and shut the door to his crypt.

"'Once the sorcerer was sealed into his tomb, the dragons on the island suddenly began to attack. The people, fearing they'd be hurt, and believing the island to be an evil place haunted by his ghost, left Dragon Island never to return. No one goes there now and...'"

Al read on silently, then said, "It seems the prince knew how to get back to the island, and it says here that he followed a map and returned there." He flipped through the remaining pages. "But there's no map in this book."

"Well, I reckon the story's a clue, at least, to finding the treasure," said Jack. "That'll make Captain Gunner happy."

"A golden death mask," said Mahoot, reflecting on the story. His eyes lit up with adventure. "I'd love to see a mummy in a tomb covered in gold."

"What's this?" said Jack, pulling at a

bookmark he'd just noticed, sticking out from the last page. "There's something written on it: 'What moves on four legs, then two legs, then three legs?'"

"That's easy enough," said Al. "A person. A baby crawls, a man walks, and an old man uses a walking stick. But why would anyone leave this in the book?"

"Maybe it's a clue to the Dragon Island Treasure?" said Jack.

"But what about these numbers?" asked Mahoot.

Al looked at the bookmark. Next to the question, someone had written '7D, 120L, 42'. Al thought for a while, then replied, "We're in a study full of shelves and books. The code must relate to them somehow ... Maybe what we need to do is find a book about man, or the ages of man, or the history of man and the letters and numbers will tell us where to find it. 7D could mean we should look seven shelves down; 120L might mean count 120 books to the left; and 42 could tell us the page number."

The boys counted quickly and discovered a large volume called *The Human History*. Within minutes they were holding a map of Dragon Island.

Demon Dan and the Dragon Diamond

Many years before Al and Jack had come
to the Dragon Blood Islands, an evil pirate,
Demon Dan, crewed for Vicious Victor on
his ship. Dan's cruelty and greed were second
to none, so Victor promoted him, giving him
a ship and a rare black diamond as thanks for
his years of loyal service.

The black diamond's glittering fire fascinated Dan so he took to wearing it as an earring. It was then he began to dream of becoming the richest man in the world.

As time went on, many a treasure ship fell to Dan's demonic attacks and, with each passing year, he became greedier and nastier until even his own crew hated him. "He's the worst pirate captain ever," complained Dan's first mate. "And he never gives us our dues."

As the treasure in the ship's hold grew heavier, the first mate roused the pirate crew into a murderous mutiny.

And so, one morning, when Demon Dan came on deck, he found his ruthless cut-throats waving their weapons. "Capt'n Dan!" called the first mate. "Stand down or we'll have your guts for garters!"

"We're fed up!" cried another brigand. "You haven't shared the plunder!"

"Scurvy dogs!" Captain Dan shouted. "Go

back to your duties or I'll make you walk the plank."

"All of us? Impossible!" said a heavily scarred man.

"Pirate law demands you treat us fair!" shouted another.

"Pirate law!" yelled their captain. "You're on my boat and they're my laws. No man's taking my treasure."

One of the crew levelled his musket. "Fine. You've given us no alternative: we're taking over the ship!" he bellowed. The gun boomed, the shot wounding Dan in the chest.

The demon pirate shook himself, stepped forward and smiled, his black diamond earring glinting evilly. He pulled his sword and leapt among his mutinous crew, slashing at them in fury.

Some pirates grabbed muskets as their captain attacked single-handedly, while others fell upon Dan, brutally stabbing him with knives and swords. But the captain barely flinched from their blows and ruthlessly cut down all who stood against him.

When Dan finally cornered the last terrified members of his crew, they threw down their weapons and begged mercy from their deathless captain. Their reward was to walk the plank at the end of his sword.